THE
STOLEN
WEEKEND

Fern began her career in television in 1980. In 1994, she became the presenter of *Ready, Steady, Cook* which led to her presenting the iconic ITV flagship show *This Morning*. Fern's warmth, humour, empathy and compassion have made her incredibly popular and she has become a much sought-after presenter and is now a *Sunday Times* best-selling novelist. Fern is deeply committed to a number of charities, in particular the Genesis Research Trust founded by Professor Robert Winston to help create healthy families.

She lives with her husband Phil Vickery, the well-respected chef, and her four children in Buckinghamshire.

By the same author:

Fern: My Story

New Beginnings
Hidden Treasures
The Holiday Home
A Seaside Affair

Fern Britton

THE STOLEN WEEKEND

HARPER

HarperCollins*Publishers*
77–85 Fulham Palace Road,
Hammersmith, London W6 8JB

www.harpercollins.co.uk

Published by HarperCollins*Publishers* 2014

A catalogue record for this book
is available from the British Library

ISBN: 978-0-00-759536-5

Set in Birka by Palimpsest Book Production Limited,
Falkirk, Stirlingshire

Printed and bound in Great Britain by
Clays Ltd, St Ives plc

MIX
Paper from
responsible sources
FSC™
www.fsc.org
FSC® C007454

1

'What on earth?' Penny Leighton grappled at the side of her bed, trying to locate her mobile phone as it rang loudly somewhere close by. She blinked, bleary-eyed, at the blue fascia of her iPhone 5 as it flashed insistently at her in the darkness of the bedroom. The usually jaunty, old-fashioned ringtone was the last thing she wanted to hear at six in the morning. This morning in particular. *Who the hell was ringing her at this ungodly hour?*

Penny sat bolt upright in bed as she saw the caller's name appear.

'Audrey bloody Tipton!!' Penny angrily pressed the silent button and shoved the vibrating phone back under her pillow.

'What is that woman pestering me for now?' Penny turned over in the bed, directing the question to where her husband Simon ought to be, but was surprised to see that his side of the bed was empty. The Right Reverend Simon Canter, vicar of Pendruggan, was normally an early riser, as members of the clergy tended to be, but she hadn't anticipated that he would have got up at this unearthly hour. After all, it was a Tuesday, no early services today, and last night they'd both got to bed late. Penny was the sole owner of Penny Leighton Productions, a successful TV production company that had a string of prime-time successes under its belt. Her latest hit was a TV show called *Mr Tibbs*, based on the mystery stories of Mavis Carew. The series was filmed in and around Pendruggan, a small, unspoilt Cornish village that Penny had discovered when her best friend Helen Merrifield decided to make a fresh start there after divorcing her philandering husband. Penny had come for a visit and ended up finding not only the perfect location for *Mr Tibbs* but the man she wanted to spend the rest of her life with. Though she would never have imagined herself as a vicar's wife, she'd never been happier. Her loving and gentle husband with his chocolate-brown eyes and soft-spoken voice had brought out the best in Penny and she had no regrets about upping sticks to move to Cornwall. Or at least, not until this morning.

Knowing that Simon was up and about, Penny found it impossible to settle back to sleep. She swung her legs out of the bed and reached for her satin dressing gown, which was hanging on a peg nearby. Then she went to the window and pulled open the heavy curtains, which kept out even the most persistent sunshine.

It was April and the sky was still tinged with the night, but the purple and pink fingertips of dawn were already starting to snake their way across the horizon.

'Mmm. Red sky in the morning,' Penny observed. 'Looks like bad weather. Again.'

She trudged down the stairs to find that the house was in total darkness, except for Simon's study, where a gentle light emanated from under the doorway.

Penny knocked softly and popped her head around the door.

'Morning, Vicar.'

Simon's head was head was buried in what appeared

to be the parish appointments diary. Penny could tell from the way his fingertips were pressed against his furrowed brow that he was feeling harassed.

'Oh, good morning, darling.' He looked up from his desk, blinking at her through his glasses. 'Sorry, did I wake you?'

'I'm not sure it is quite morning yet,' Penny replied. 'And no, it wasn't you who woke me, it was a phone call from that busybody, Audrey Tipton.'

'Really, what did she want?'

'Dunno – I cut her off.' Penny looked down at her iPhone. 'But it looks as though she left me a message.'

'You should be having a lie-in. You look done in.'

'I feel done in. The last few weeks have been really gruelling. I'm so exhausted, I couldn't even enjoy the wrap party.'

'I'm sorry you had to go alone, darling, but there was so much to do here,' he sighed guiltily.

Penny walked over to her husband and gave his balding head a kiss. 'Oh, stuff that. You didn't miss anything: it was only the usual shenanigans. The lead actors all lording it over each other and getting pissed while the runners and researchers snogged one another.' She peered at the papers spread over his desk. 'What's the problem? Is there anything I can do to help?'

Simon put down his pen, took off his glasses and ran a hand anxiously over his shining scalp. 'It's this whole business with the new vicar at St Peter's.'

The church of St Peter's was in Trevay, the nearest town and a thriving seaside resort. It had been without its own vicar for months and Simon had been asked by the bishop to help out with services until a suitable candidate was found to fill the post. As if it wasn't enough having two congregations to minister to, Simon was also expected to supervise the builders carrying out restorations to St Peter's bell tower. As a result, the last few weeks had been as gruelling for him as they had for Penny. They'd barely had a moment to themselves and were both exhausted.

'The verger at St Peter's Church has been taken ill,' Simon told her. 'He's been a godsend, helping me out with the services and keeping things ticking over. Without him, I just don't know how I'm going to cope. We've got two funerals scheduled tomorrow morning – one here and one in Trevay – at the same time, so I'm going to have to phone around and find someone to officiate.' He looked up at her despairingly. 'And it doesn't end there. Until the verger recovers, I'll have to cut evensong down here so that I can dash over to Trevay to take the six p.m. service, and then there's—'

Penny laid a gentle hand on his shoulder. 'Have you told the bishop? Surely he can sort something out?'

'I called the diocese secretary yesterday, but the bishop is on a retreat until next week. I probably won't see him until he shows up to bless the new bell tower. There's so much to organise, but I already feel as if I've been pulled in half – there's only so much of me to go round.' Simon's pinched face was etched with worry. Penny's heart went out to her beleaguered husband.

'Oh, Simon. Poor you. Have you even had a cup of tea yet?'

He shook his head.

'Well,' said Penny, giving Simon an encouraging smile, 'ecclesiastical matters may not be my forte, but I do know how to boil a kettle.'

*

Later that morning, at a more civilised hour, Penny knelt on the sofa in the cosy sitting room at the vicarage. From this vantage point, she was able to see the last of the trucks loading up the dismantled sets of the *Mr Tibbs* shoot. The set was a painstaking reconstruction of Fifties village life, strategically placed in front of a terrace of Sixties council houses whose occupants were well compensated for the inconvenience. All in all, everyone was happy: the TV crew did their utmost to keep disruption to a minimum; the actors mingled cordially with the residents; locals and visitors alike came to watch the location shoots and the popularity of the series had given tourism in the area a much-needed boost. There was little conflict, but the occasional voice of dissent could sometimes be heard.

It was usually the same voice.

Penny held the phone away from her ear as Audrey gave vent to her feelings.

'The success of your programme owes everything to the co-operation of we, the villagers! Without us, *Mr Tibbs* would be a complete failure, Mrs Canter!'

Penny took a deep breath. She'd already been listening to Audrey for ten minutes. Apparently, the woman's neurotic, smelly and aged cocker spaniels had been disturbed by the crew dismantling the set early this morning, hence the dawn phone call.

'Yes, Audrey, we do everything we can to avoid disturbing anyone, but if the crew leave it any later there's a risk the trucks could hold up through traffic at rush hour, or what passes for rush hour in this part of the world.'

It took another ten minutes of yes, Audreys, no Audreys, and three-bags-full, Audreys before Penny was able to get her off the subject and onto another one. But predictably, even then, it was an unwelcome topic.

'So, as vicar's wife, it is incumbent upon you to represent the qualities of charitable benevolence, which is why the Old People's Christmas Luncheon Committee have nominated you as chairperson. Our first meeting will be held in the church hall tomorrow at five p.m., we will expect you there.'

'What?!' Penny couldn't believe her ears. 'Who nominated me? I'll have you know that I've given myself two weeks' holiday after a very long and punishing shoot. I've no intention of doing anything other than putting my feet up!'

'The *committee* nominated you.'

'Who's on the committee?'

'Geoffrey and I, of course, and Emma Scott – Pendruggan's Brown Owl. It's a great honour for you. And it's not merely a token role, either. Your task will be to drum up support. The Old People's Christmas Luncheon is a village institution. The old folks rely on it.'

'But it's only April.' Penny said, weakly.

'December will come around sooner than you think. Tomorrow at five p.m., remember.' And with that, Audrey rang off, leaving Penny under a cloud of doom.

*

Helen Merrifield was feeling damp, cold and miserable. Cornwall had just endured its wettest and wildest winter on record, and while Pendruggan had got off lightly compared to many of the coastal communities, it hadn't emerged completely unscathed. The lovely, cosy charm of

Helen's old farmworker's cottage, Gull's Cry, had been severely compromised by the constant deluge of rain. The tiny, slow trickle that had started in one corner of her bathroom had turned into a steady drip-drip, the drips multiplying with each fresh rainfall until the upstairs ceilings were a patchwork of weeping stains and the bedroom floors were littered with pots and pans and buckets.

'Piran! Come and look at this – the one in the bathroom is definitely getting worse!'

Piran Ambrose was Helen's boyfriend and the epitome of brooding masculinity. They'd been together for a while, but they didn't live together. Both valued their independence and knew that sharing a house would drive them nuts. Much of the time Helen found his dark and mercurial nature quite thrilling, but it could also be a blooming pain the arse. This was one of those pain-in-the-arse moments.

His deep Cornish bass reverberated up the stairs. ''Aven't got time. Gotta dash.'

This was immediately followed by the clatter of buckets being overturned as Helen came dashing out of the bathroom and down the stairs. She managed to catch him before the front door of the cottage had creaked fully open.

'Where are you going? You promised me that someone would come out to have a look at it. That was days ago and we're still waiting.'

'Think you're the only one with a leaky roof? There's plenty worse off than you, maid, and I can't be expected to sit twiddling my thumbs, waiting!'

'So I have sit around and twiddle mine! But of course, my time isn't important, unlike Piran Ambrose, historian of note!'

Piran frowned at the sarcasm in her voice. 'What

exactly have you got to do that is more important than my job?'

'Er . . .' Helen faltered momentarily, but then rallied: 'I promised to run Queenie down to the surgery later. Her bunions are playing up.' She jutted her chin out defiantly.

'Bunions, eh? Really? How taxing for you.' Piran was quite good at sarcasm himself when it suited. 'Look, maid, we're talking about the discovery of a Roman fort here! This is the most significant find Cornwall's seen in decades – and it's only two miles from my own doorstep. Opportunities like that don't come along very often in a historian's life. The archeological team need all the local support they can get. The bad weather has hampered the dig and they've got to work quickly if the site isn't going to be washed away by more bad weather.'

Piran and Helen stood at the door and looked out at the ominous sky.

'But what about me and the cottage? Aren't we in danger of being washed away too?' she asked plaintively.

Piran shook his headed and headed off towards his car, speaking as he went: 'Look, I've asked Gasping Bob to come out, He should be here later.'

'Who?' Helen shouted after him.

'Gasping Bob!' And with that, Piran climbed into his pickup and sped off.

'For some reason,' Helen said to herself, 'that name doesn't inspire me with confidence.'

*

'Where's my phone?' Simon's panicked voice carried through the hallway and upstairs to where Penny was hunting for some ibuprofen in the bathroom cabinet. She was finding it impossible to wind down. Even though the shoot was over, the phone hadn't stopped ringing with requests and queries for Simon. His stress levels were starting to get to her now. She'd slept badly and had a throbbing pain in her shoulder, not to mention the remnants of a hangover.

'By the front door, on the sideboard,' she shouted back, riffling through the packets of aspirin, indigestion remedies and vitamin C tablets.

Moments later, another anxious shout: 'My car keys, where are they? I just had them in my hand.'

'Oh, for heaven's sake!' Penny gave up her fruitless search and headed downstairs. She found Simon anxiously hopping from foot to foot. 'Where did you have them last?'

'Just now!' His voice was a strangled screech.

'Calm down, darling. They won't have gone far.'

Penny's eyes spied his Nokia, still on the sideboard, and next to it a set of keys.

'Here you are, Simon. You must have put them both down when you put your coat on. Now, is that everything?'

'Er . . . not sure, possibly not. Look, I've got to go – I've should have been at St Peter's ten minutes ago! Bye.'

He planted a distracted peck on her cheek and then dashed out the door.

As the house settled into silence, Penny let out a sigh of relief. 'Right, now for half an hour on the sofa with a hot-water bottle on my shoulder.'

Switching her mobile phone off, Penny boiled a kettle, filled her hot-water bottle with its Paddington Bear cover – tatty and much loved since childhood – and headed off to put her feet up. She'd no sooner arranged herself on the sofa than the doorbell rang. Penny pretended not to hear it. It rang again. More insistently this time.

'Bother, bother, bother.'

Penny launched herself from the sofa and stomped down the corridor. She threw open the door, ready to tell whoever it was to bugger off, but managed to bite back on the words when she found herself confronted by the toothless grin of Queenie Quintrel.

Normally Penny would have been delighted to welcome the ancient Cockney proprietress of the village store, but right now she wasn't it the mood. She offered a tight smile. 'Queenie. What an unexpected pleasure.'

Queenie had run the village store for longer than anyone could remember. An evacuee from London during the war, she'd stayed on and married a local man. She'd never lost her accent, and her outspoken manner and blue rinse were as famous as the home-made pasties she sold in her shop.

'Wotcha, Pen. Ain't you expecting me?' An untipped fag dangled between her lips, its blue smoke wisping its way into the Vicarage.

This left Penny on the back foot. 'Er, should I be?'

'Yeah! You ain't forgot, 'ave yer?'

'Possibly.'

'The Great Pendruggan Bake-Off, ain't it! Raising money for the St Morwenna's Respite Home for the Elderly. We're all supposed to be making something and you and me was gonna be a team, remember?'

Penny's heart sank. Yes, she did remember now. How could this have come around so quickly?

'But I thought that was months away?'

Queenie gave one of her trademark cackles. 'Well, it

was months away, months ago! I did tell Simon to remind you I was coming round today when I saw him at church on Sunday.'

'He's got so much on his mind, he must have forgotten. Does it have to be today? You see, I've . . .'

Queenie wasn't taking no for an answer. 'It's gotta be today. I've got Simple Tony in, minding the shop for a couple of hours, but you know what 'e's like! Anyway, the first round of judging is tomorrow and we're on. Dontcha remember, we've called ourselves "The Best of the West". I'm doing the best of Cornwall with my Cornish pasty pie and you're doing the best of London with those little puff-pastry cheesecakes, Richmond Maids of Honour.'

'But I haven't done any shopping . . . the ingredients . . . the recipes . . .?'

'Never you mind about that, dearie. I've got all we need in this little bag of tricks.' Queenie stood aside to reveal a bulging tartan shopping bag on wheels, fit to bursting with bags of flours and other sundry items.

'Now shove out the way. We'd better get a move on.'

Penny stood aside as Queenie wheeled all before her. Her shoulders sagged, as she felt all resistance drain away – along with any hope of five minutes' peace.

2

Helen ended up waiting in all day for 'Gasping Bob'. Despite leaving him numerous messages, there had been no word from Piran. Presumably he'd been so absorbed in his Roman fort that he'd forgotten all about her. That evening, the storm took a nasty turn as another weather front settled in over the region. Helen made her way up to bed with a strong sense of foreboding about what the latest bout of wind and rain would do to her little cottage. She slept fitfully and was already awake when a large chunk of her bedroom ceiling caved in, the water cascading down the flaking plaster and all over her John Lewis symmetric weave, thick-pile rug.

Not normally given to crying, she sat in stunned silence and surveyed the wreckage of what used to be her bedroom. Feeling the hot well of tears threatening to bubble over, Helen realised she had reached some sort of breaking point. Grabbing her dressing gown, she made her way down to the front door and pulled on her wellies. Within minutes she'd jumped into her little car and driven the short distance to Piran's house. It took a few angry thumps on the old wooden front door before his gruff voice could be heard from within.

'All right, keep your ruddy 'air on. Where's the fire?'

The words died in his mouth as he took in the vision of his usually elegant and graceful girlfriend. Sopping

13

wet and looking like she'd been dragged through a hedge backwards, Helen fired out her words like short, sharp pistol shots.

'If I have to suffer one more night of Chinese water torture in my own home, I, Helen Merrifield, am personally going to beat you, Piran Ambrose, to death' – she yanked a sodden and muddy welly from one foot – 'with this Wellington boot!!' She brandished it at him.

For a moment Piran could only stand there in his hastily pulled on boxers, gawping at her. Then he collapsed into gales of helpless laughter. Helen promptly burst into tears and Piran scooped her up, took her inside and then tucked her up in his bed.

*

It was now Thursday morning and Helen was watching slightly aghast as a man of indeterminate age, but somewhere between eighty-five and one hundred and five years old hoisted a ladder from the top of a battered white van and staggered towards the door of Gull's Cry. His wispy grey hair was tied back in a ponytail, he wore the tightest of skimpy shorts that showcased the knobbliest of brown knees. He was wearing a T-shirt bearing the legend *Cornish Men Do It Slowly* and a brown roll-up poked out of the side of his mouth.

'This is Gasping Bob? The man who's going to fix my roof?' she whispered to Piran, incredulous.

'Don't judge a book by its cover, maid.'

Piran greeted Gasping Bob like a long-lost friend and Helen was surprised to see the old man shoot up the ladder and on to the roof with the agility of a geriatric Tarzan.

Moments later, he'd assessed the damage and was back down again.

'Well, what do you think?' asked Helen.

Gasping Bob shook his head and said, 'Ah . . .'

'Is that good news or bad news?'

He shook his head, shrugged his shoulders and said, 'Ah . . .'

'Well, are you going to fix it?'

'Ah . . .'

Helen turned to Piran. 'Please tell me that this man is going to fix my roof. I don't think I can take much more of this.'

Piran looked at her with irritation. 'Leave the man to do his work and stop wittering, woman.' And with that, he and Gasping Bob wandered off in a huddle and carried on their private conversation in what sounded to Helen like more ahs and umms.

Helen balled her fists in annoyance. 'Bloody Cornwall! Bloody Cornish men!'

And with that she headed off across the village green to the vicarage in hope of finding a cup of tea, or something stronger.

*

'So, you're camping out at Piran's until further notice then?' Penny poured them each a cup of tea from the shiny brown tea pot and offered her friend a chocolate HobNob.

'Looks that way, but we'll drive each other nuts after a few days. He can't bear to have a woman cluttering up the place and he's impossible to live with – just so bloody male, and Cornish male to boot.' Helen sipped her tea. 'Got anything stronger?'

'Brandy? Can't join you – Simon's car is playing up again and I'll have to pick him up in Trevay.'

'No fun tippling on your own,' Helen responded. 'What about you – you look exhausted?'

'I am. It's been one thing after another. What with the shoot, then Simon's stress levels, plus the whole village contriving to drive us into an early grave . . . I spent most of yesterday baking with Queenie for this Pendruggan Bake-Off thingummy and then, to top it all, we only went and won the first heat.'

'Congratulations!' Helen registered the thunderous look on Penny's face. 'Aren't you pleased?'

'Pleased? That's the last thing I needed! Now I'll have to go through the whole blooming thing again next week. There's four heats and then a grand final, with Mary Berry herself coming to judge. Still, it'll be a lovely feeling if we beat Audrey Tipton. That woman is the bane of my life.'

'Oh yes, very satisfying.'

'All I want to do is to crawl into bed and shut the world away. The post-production of *Mr Tibbs* will be a walk in the park compared to this lot. Living in Pendruggan can sometimes feel like being beaten to death with a tea cosy!'

The two friends nibbled on their HobNobs glumly.

'Wait a minute! I've had an idea.' There was an excited gleam in Penny's eye. 'I got a call from the director of *Mr Tibbs* today. We're all supposed to be having a break before post-production starts, but he told me there are a few problems with the sound quality and he's getting David Cunningham to come to the dubbing studios to re-do a couple of things.'

Helen nodded, wondering where this was leading.

'David's only free for a few days before he moves on to a new project, so they're recording this weekend,'

Penny continued, her voice bubbling with excitement. 'While they don't *need* me, strictly speaking I should be on hand to make sure all goes well. Which gives me the perfect excuse to nip up to London for the weekend. All I'd have to do is literally pop my head in to make sure that everything's tickety-boo – once I've done that, we can have the whole weekend to ourselves. What do you think?'

Helen sat up and clapped her hands together.

'London! Oh, Pen, that would be just the tonic we both need. Cornwall's lovely, but right now, I could just do with a bit of an urban fix. Pizza Express!'

'Yes!' said Penny. 'Twenty-four-hour corner shops that sell everything from corn plasters to condoms!'

'Harvey Nicks, Selfridges, M&S!' Helen said gleefully. 'And I'm sure we could squeeze in dinner at Chez Walter. I've such a craving for their slow-roasted pork belly!'

'I'm a sucker for their venison cottage pie, myself.' Penny grabbed her friend's hand conspiratorially. 'We could even have a night at Mortimer's.'

'Oh, God! Champagne cocktails to die for, in the heart of Mayfair! Let's go now, now, now!'

Suddenly the excitement evaporated from Penny's face and she slumped back in her seat. 'Hang on, what about Simon? He's really under the cosh at the moment. It would be too awful if I left him to it.'

'Oh, come off it, Simon's got loads of help. What about the blue-rinse brigade? They always muck in, don't they? And it's only for a couple of nights. Piran will be glad to get rid of me and my constant nagging.'

'I'm not so sure about Simon. We all agree that I'm not the greatest vicar's wife, but he does rely on me. The trouble is, I've had it up to here with it all.' She waved a hand above her head. 'If I don't get away, I'm afraid our marriage will suffer. Is that terribly selfish of me?'

'Of course it isn't.' Helen gave her friend an encouraging smile. 'You do more for Simon than you realise: you keep him on the straight and narrow; you're his gatekeeper, holding all the busybodies at bay. You've just worked twelve weeks solid, around the clock – you deserve a break.'

'I know,' said Penny, miserably. 'But I'm not sure Simon will agree.'

*

'But the timing is terrible.' Simon's face was full of consternation. He had been in the study, working on his sermons for the coming weekend's services, when Penny had come in to broach the subject of going away. His reaction had been much as she'd expected.

'I know. But they really can't manage without me,' she said guiltily, knowing it was a fib. 'It's my job to be there,' she added, which at least was technically true.

'Well, I'll just have to manage without you then. I'm sure that some of the other villagers will help out here in Pendruggan.'

'Of course they will, darling. They've never let you down.' Unlike me, she thought.

'But you will be back here on Tuesday, in time for the blessing of the bell tower?'

'Yes, Simon, I'll make sure we're home by then.'

'*We?*' Simon raised his eyebrows questioningly.

'Oh, Helen and I are travelling together – didn't I mention it?'

'No, you didn't.' Simon's face was suddenly serious. 'I

realise that you have your own life, Penny, but being a vicar's wife is important too.'

Penny felt a hot flush of shame creep up her neck, but she needed a break, dammit. Couldn't he see that? It wasn't as if she was running off to join the bloody circus!

'Simon, I promise, I'll be home on Sunday. It's just a quick hop. You'll hardly even notice I've gone.'

She gave him a hug that was returned only reluctantly.

Leaving Simon to his sermons, she closed the study door, tiptoed down the hall and then did a little dance for joy. Despite the pangs of guilt, the prospect of her forthcoming great escape filled her with euphoria.

She sent a text to Helen:

Pack that Mulberry weekend bag. I'm booking us on tonight's sleeper. Bring wine! Px

3

Penny and Helen arrived at Truro station in good time to rendezvous with their overnight-sleeper train to London Paddington.

'What a complete stroke of genius this is!' remarked Helen. 'I've never been on a sleeper before.'

'The last time I went on one was over twenty years ago,' replied Penny as they climbed aboard the waiting train. 'Went to Cornwall for the summer while I was at uni. Got myself a job in a pub in Newquay. Beach all day, worked like a Trojan until the pub shut, then went clubbing every night. Had a ball.'

'Holiday romance?' Helen's eyes twinkled.

'A few.' Penny winked. 'One really hot lifeguard called Merlin. He had loads of other girls on the go too, of course, but I didn't care. I just wanted some fun.'

'Fun – that's all we girls want, right?'

'Right!' Penny agreed. 'Especially this weekend. But first we need to find our compartment.'

They wandered up the corridor. 'Ah, here we are!' Penny stopped outside their berth and opened the door. Inside it was narrow, but there were two decent-sized bunks, one upper and one lower.'

'Bagsy I'm having the top one!' said Helen.

'Hey, that's not fair!'

There was an unseemly scuffle as both women

laughingly tried to throw their bags on to the top bunk. Through sheer force of will, Helen won out, but justice was delivered when she climbed ungainly up after her bag and promptly banged her head on the ceiling.

'Serves you right,' said Penny, good-naturedly.

'Oh Pen, what an adventure,' From her vantage point, Helen took in the little wash basin with its hot and cold taps. Each bunk had a snug duvet and plump pillows, and they'd each been provided with soap, a towel and a bottle of mineral water. 'It's all so dinky and sweet.'

'Yep, dinky, sweet and a bit of a tight squeeze. There's a buffet lounge with a bar down the corridor. I think we should decamp there for a bit,' said Penny.

'Another brilliant idea.'

Pausing only to grab their handbags, the two friends set off towards the bar.

*

Helen pointed her finger unsteadily at her friend. 'You look pished. Your eyes have shtarted to go.'

'I'm perfectly sober.' Penny waggled her head equally unsteadily. 'You're mishtaken, me ol' mucker. It is you who is pished. I mean pissed.'

The women giggled loudly, and for longer than was strictly necessary, drawing attention from the adjoining table. Seated at it was serious-looking middle-aged man, who clearly disapproved. He gave a loud tut.

'I'm sorry? Did you say something?' Penny peered at him over the rim of her plastic glass. Two hours ago, they'd bought themselves a sandwich and a teensy bottle of red wine, from which they would each get approximately one small glass each. In front of them on the Formica table now lay the detritus of their half-eaten prawn mayo sandwiches plus eight teensy wine bottles.

Without a word, the tutting man closed the tablet he was reading and stood to leave.

'Was it something we said?' Helen asked innocently.

The man tutted again but avoided their eyes as he made his way back to his own compartment.

'Men!' said Helen, with feeling. 'Bet he's bloody Cornish too.'

'Don't get us started on Cornwall and Cornish men again! We've worked out that you can't get a Cornish man to do anything in a hurry.'

'They don't like it!' Helen concurred, loudly.

'And,' Penny added, narrowing her eyes, 'they really don't like women taking charge.'

'No, except possibly in the bedroom,' Helen sniggered.

'I'm serious!'

'So am I. You've got to admit it, Pen. Cornish men are very, very sexy.'

'What about Gasping Bob? Was he sexy?'

'Well . . .'

Penny never got to find out what Helen thought of Gasping Bob's sexiness or otherwise because the reply was drowned out by the stewardess pulling down the grille and hanging a closed sign on the bar.

'Sorry, ladies. We're shutting up for the night.' She smiled over at them.

Penny and Helen surveyed the empty bottles in front of them.

'Time for beddywed,' said Penny.

Helen rose to her feet, swaying rather dangerously.

Penny did the same and the two women linked arms as they made their way, rather erratically, towards the door. They thanked the stewardess and gave her a wave before making their way out. The exit clearly wasn't wide enough for both of them to leave side-by-side, but they tried it anyway. As Helen collided with the doorframe, she let out another loud snigger.

'Ssssh, people are trying to sleep you know!' came a muffled voice from behind one of the compartments.

'Bet that's Mr Grumpy,' whispered Helen loudly.

Eventually, after much banging and crashing, they made it back to their compartment. Getting undressed and washed was a rather messy affair, but eventually they were both in their cosy nightclothes.

'That's not a onesie you're wearing, is it?' asked Helen.

'Onesie's aren't just for kids, you know,' said Penny, peeking out from underneath her rabbit ears, one of which had fallen over her left eye, giving her quite a comical look.

'Simon hasn't seen you like that, has he?'

'Simon loves me no matter what I look like in bed.'

Helen raised a drunken eyebrow. 'I'll take your word for it.'

Too squiffy to care what anyone thought, Penny crawled into her lower bunk, pulling the warm duvet up to her neck.

'Aren't you going to give me a leg up?'

Penny opened one bleary eye and looked up at Helen. 'Eh?'

Helen stuck her bottom lip out. 'I can't get up there. It's like climbing Kilimanjaro.'

Penny thought about it for a moment.

'Pwetty please?' said Helen hopefully, but her face

fell as Penny turned over and was soon snoring like a train.

*

The first thought that occurred to Helen as she emerged from unconsciousness the following morning was that someone had stuck her eyelids together with glue. The second was that the incessant bang, bang, banging wasn't the thudding of her heart or the hammering of her headache, but was in fact, somebody banging loudly on the door of the compartment.

She tried to prop herself up on her elbows but as her eyes gradually opened and took in the scene around her, she saw that next to her head were two feet recognisable as Penny's by the bunny rabbit toes of her onesie.

She gave one of the big toes a hard squeeze.

'Wake up,' she croaked. 'Someone's at the door.'

The only response was a muffled groan from the other end of the cramped bottom berth. Helen slowly got out of the bed, wincing as a shooting pain pierced her temple. Gingerly she picked her way over the untidy piles of clothes and bags and opened the door. Outside was a fresh-faced young steward.

'I'm terribly sorry to disturb you, madam, but we've reached Paddington. I've been banging on the door for ages. I was just about to get the master key to gain access. We thought something might have happened.'

Helen, patted her hair in a futile attempt to restore order to what she knew must be her rather dishevelled appearance.

'I'm dreadfully sorry. We seem to have overslept.'

'Heavy night, was it?'

Helen feigned indignation. 'Not in the slightest. The motion of the train must have given us a deeper sleep than usual. That's all.'

The young man looked at her doubtfully. 'People often get carried away on the sleeper, but then they forget what an early arrival we have.'

'Well, we'll just get washed and dressed—'

The young man shook his head. 'There's no time for that, I'm afraid. We've been here ages and you've got to leave by seven a.m. It's already well past that and we can't wait any longer. I'm sorry, but we have to turn the train around or else we'll be in hot water.'

'You mean we have to go *now*?'

''Fraid so.'

'Oh.'

'I'll wait here and help you with your things. There's showers and . . . um . . . facilities on the concourse. You can use them.'

'Er . . .'

But there was no time for arguing. The corridor outside their compartment was bustling with people doing useful things and outside their door a smiling cleaner was waiting expectantly with a J-cloth and a mop in her hands. Once Penny was apprised of the situation, she shuffled out of bed and the two women gathered themselves together as best as they could. There was no time to change out of their nightwear or to arrange themselves and within moments, they were hustled off the train with friendly thank-yous and helpful directions towards the Ladies.

Juggling their coats and bags, Penny and Helen blinked and looked around them. After the cocoon of the train, Paddington station was a hive of activity. All around them, commuters swarmed from trains like ants. The platforms were filled with passengers all coming and going. It was dizzying, and in their present condition they were finding it quite a challenge to orient themselves.

'Where did he say the loos were?' Helen peered uncertainly across the concourse, her hungover brain still confused by all of the activity.

Penny was just about to say that she had spotted the sign for the Ladies when they were approached by a young man with a kindly face. He thrust something into Penny's hand.

'It's not much, but it'll cover the price of a cuppa.' He patted her hand sympathetically before hurrying off down towards the sign for the London Underground.

Penny looked at her palm and saw two shiny pound coins. They looked at each other in astonishment.

'You don't think he thought we were . . .?'

'Bag ladies!!'

'Come on, let's get dressed before we attract any more attention,' Helen said, grabbing Penny's arm and steering her towards the loos.

*

Ignoring more curious stares, they washed and dressed hurriedly and were soon heading towards central London in a black cab.

'Can we please pretend that incident never happened?' said Penny, looking much more respectable in a smart red Burberry mac, though she hid her eyes behind a pair of Dior sunglasses.

Helen feigned nonchalance. 'Pretend what never happened?'

They sped along the Marylebone Road. The route along the Westway was lined with new developments of luxury flats and offices.

'London always seems to be one giant building site.' observed Penny. 'It's forever changing.'

'Unlike Pendruggan, which is always the same,' replied Helen. 'Queenie's had the same display of faded postcards and out-of-date Cornish fudge in her window since the seventies.'

Before long they were driving up Monmouth Street, where the cabbie dropped them outside their boutique hotel, The Hanborough.

'Thank God!' exclaimed Penny. 'Civilisation.'

The hotel was the epitome of luxurious London cool. The foyer was a white oasis of calm; low-slung chaises longues were dotted across the marbled Italianate floor and giant bowls of burnished bronze showcased opulent arrangements of orchids, hyacinths and lavender.

After checking in, they made their way up to their rooms, which were next door to each other on the fifth floor. Agreeing to rendezvous at 1 p.m. for lunch, they went their separate ways.

Helen dumped her bags on her king-size bed decked out in Egyptian cotton. Her room mirrored the rest of the hotel with its white walls, curtains, bedding and minimalist white furniture. She headed over to the window and took in the view of the vibrant London scene spread out before her. The morning rush had died down and on the street below she could see hip, young media types sauntering leisurely between their hip offices and equally hip coffee shops.

She closed the curtains against the bright spring sunshine, kicked off her Kurt Geiger heels and flaked out on the bed.

*

'God, I love this place!' eulogised Penny when they met in the foyer at lunchtime.

'Me too,' said Helen, 'Did you check out the Cowshed toiletries in the bathroom? The soap is to die for!'

'I know, I've already made inroads into them. Sat in the roll-top bath for an hour with a scented candle. Heavenly.'

'What now? I'm famished.'

'Me too.'

'What I really fancy is an American Hot with extra mushrooms at Pizza Express.' Helen's mouth was watering at the thought of it. 'Dean Street is only ten minutes' walk. Let's head over.'

'Ah,' said Penny, 'sorry to disappoint, but I've arranged to meet Neil, the new director, at my club on Wardour Street.'

Helen's face fell. 'Not work?'

'Honestly, it'll only be for half an hour. He'll fill me in on what's going on and then I won't have to go to the studios.'

Helen didn't look convinced.

'Look, I promise it won't take long – and they do a mean cheese-and-jalapeno burger there. And an even meaner Bloody Mary.'

Helen relented. 'OK, but you're paying, Penny Leighton Productions.'

'It'll be our pleasure.'

*

They strolled leisurely through Seven Dials, stopping to window-shop in the many trendy clothes shops, and were soon on Shaftesbury Avenue heading towards Penny's Club, The House, on Dean Street.

Situated in an elegant Georgian townhouse, the discreet entranceway led to maze of private meeting rooms, bars, and a restaurant that played host to the great and good of London Medialand. Some of the country's most famous actors, playwrights, directors and journalists were members – and membership was both exclusive and expensive.

As they entered, Helen noticed that Stephen Fry was just leaving. The concierge, who recognised Penny, greeted her like an old friend and ushered them into the main bar area, which was a decked out in a cleverly realised shabby-chic style that had probably cost millions. Penny spotted Neil immediately; he was sitting on one of the antique Chesterfield sofas that were dotted around the room. The large informal space was peopled by a fairly equal mix of men and women, some in small groups, others on their own, working on their iPads or MacAirs. The room was dominated by a central bar which ran the whole length of it, and adjoining the bar area was a restaurant. Both restaurant and bar were full and buzzing during the busy lunch period.

'Hi, Neil!'

Neil, a handsome blond in his thirties, stood and gave Penny a big hug.

'You remember Helen, my friend from Pendruggan?'

'I don't want to get in your way,' said Helen, 'so I'll go and sit at the bar while you two catch up.'

'Thanks, Helen,' said Penny. 'Hopefully this won't take long – right, Neil?'

Neil gave her a reassuring smile. 'Everything's fine – just need to run a couple of things by you.'

Helen left them to it and headed over to the bar. It was busy, but she could see a couple who were just vacating their seats and she popped herself onto one of them as they departed.

Despite the full bar, she was served immediately by a bright and breezy barman.

'What can I get you?'

'Not sure. What's good today?'

'Depends. What sort of mood you in?'

'Feel like being nice to myself.'

'Then I've got the perfect drink for being nice to yourself – the Ambrosia. Champagne, aged cognac and triple sec, plus a few of my secret ingredients. It's named after the food of the gods – can't get nicer to yourself than that.'

'Sold!'

Helen watched as he artfully filled a cocktail shaker with ice before adding the ingredients and shaking them thoroughly. He poured the contents into a highball glass filled with more ice and topped it up with chilled champagne.

He placed the glass in front of her on a small black napkin. 'A drink fit for a goddess,' he said, giving her a cheeky smile.

'I bet you say that to all the goddesses.' She smiled cheekily back at him.

The drink certainly tasted like Ambrosia and Helen could feel the last vestiges of her hangover slip away.

She dug around in her bag and fished out her iPad. Logging into her email account she skimmed through the usual junk until she came to a brand-new photo of her granddaughter, Summer, that had been sent to her from her son, Sean. Summer was sitting in the lap of her mother Terri and was holding the soft grey elephant that Helen had bought her for Christmas. Helen had had a long visit from them in the New Year and now they were visiting Terri's family up north. Summer looked completely adorable.

In the email, Sean had written:

> Summer's favourite toy now, she won't let it out of her sight. We're calling it Ellie.

How sweet, thought Helen.

Next, she sent Piran an email:

> What you doing? I'm sitting in Pen's club. Hugh Laurie's at other end of the bar!

Helen googled Heals' website. Assuming the roof ever got fixed, and if there was any money left in her depleted coffers, she resolved to treat herself to a new rug. Maybe they'd find time to pop down there this afternoon; it wasn't far.

An email from Piran pinged back at her:

> Who is Hugh Laurie?

Honestly, thought Helen, you'd have thought he'd been living in cave for all he knew about popular culture.

> Never mind. How is the Roman Fort?

Moments later the reply:

> Muddy.

'You're a mine of information, Piran Ambrose,' she muttered under her breath.

It wasn't long before Penny said goodbye to Neil, who was heading back to the dubbing studio, and joined her friend at the bar.

'All's well, which is just what I wanted to hear.'

'Fab. I've checked with the restaurant and they think they can fit us in in ten minutes.'

'Brilliant. Time for a Bloody Mary, I think.'

'Another Ambrosia for you, Goddess?' said the cheeky barman.

'I think goddesses should stick to just one at lunchtime, don't you?'

'You're the boss.'

'Actually, make mine a virgin Bloody Mary, will, you? I don't want to push my luck,' said Penny.

No sooner were their drinks served than a waiter from the restaurant came to tell them their table was ready.

Helen was just stooping to collect her bag and coat from her feet when Penny grabbed her arm and hissed urgently, 'Don't move! He might not see us.'

Immediately Helen looked up, her eyes scanning the room. It didn't take her long to understand why Penny was keen not to be seen. But it was too late – they'd been spotted.

Coming towards them, wearing an impeccably tailored Savile Row suit and sporting an expensive hair-weave and a smarmy smile, was Quentin Clarkson. Not only was he the Chairman of TV7 – which meant he held the future of *Mr Tibbs* in his sweaty palms – but he was also Penny's ex and a grade-A slimeball.

'Penny, my dear!' he gushed, oozing insincere charm.

'Quentin, how super!' While Penny's rictus grin did a good impression of politeness as they air-kissed, her eyes as they met Helen's told an entirely different story.

4

'How perfectly marvellous to run into you! I was only saying to Miriam the other day that we really don't see enough of you.'

'Well, Quentin, I'm permanently based in Cornwall now, so I don't get up to town much.'

'Ah yes, I heard that you've buried yourself in some godforsaken backwater.'

'Hardly – it's Pendruggan, Quentin.'

His face was momentarily blank.

'The village where we film the series? *Mr Tibbs*?'

The penny dropped and Quentin gave her an unpleasant smile. 'Oh yes, that's right. It's all coming back to me now. Didn't I hear that you'd gone and married a vicar? Can't be true? Penny Leighton, the ultimate good-time girl? Oh, it's too priceless!'

Penny replied through gritted teeth: 'It suits me down to the ground. I love being among people who are so sincere. Maybe you should try it sometime?'

'Eh?' Quentin was silenced for a nanosecond before he recovered and turned his attention to Helen. 'Well, now, who's this?'

He took her hand, unbidden, and proceeded to plant a slimy kiss on it.

'Helen Merrifield. We've met before. Years ago . . .' She

wanted to add, 'when you had real hair', but resisted the temptation.

'Did we? I feel sure I'd remember someone as charming as you.'

'Well, you're pretty unforgettable yourself,' said Helen, removing her hand; he'd already held on to it far longer than she was comfortable with.

'So tell me,' he turned his attention back to Penny, 'what brings you back from the sticks?'

'I'm only here for a couple of days.'

'Business or pleasure?'

'Er . . .' Penny hesitated. While she was perfectly entitled to a break and her company was independent, she knew that Quentin was likely to be aware of the filming schedule. He wasn't her paymaster, but she didn't want him to think she wasn't putting her back into it.

'Business. Making sure *Mr Tibbs* is better than ever for TV7.'

'Well, that's just perfect! Miriam and I are throwing a drinks party tonight – you simply have to come.'

'Well, I, er . . . not sure . . .' Penny caught Helen's eyes, which were looking at her in alarm.

'Nonsense, I insist! Everyone is coming. Sir Nigel will be there, and Baroness Hardy.' Penny's heart was sinking. Sir Nigel Cameron and Baroness Hardy were co-owners of TV7; their good opinion of her and Penny Leighton Productions really mattered. Schmoozing and glad-handing was an integral part of her job. They had just wrapped the latest series of *Mr Tibbs* and securing a new one was a long way from being a done deal. It wasn't all about ratings and revenues; the goodwill of the board could spell the difference between a new contract and cancellation. The future of *Mr Tibbs* and the jobs of the actors and crew were in her hands. *The buck stops with me*, she thought, resignedly.

Helen, however had other ideas. 'She couldn't possibly, Penny's taking me out to dinner.'

Quentin Clarkson wasn't to be deterred. 'Then you must come along too – I'm sure I can offer something much more tempting than some boring old dinner.' He eyed her suggestively.

'Of course we'll come, Quentin, though we won't be able to stay too long,' conceded Penny, avoiding Helen's furious stare.

'Marvellous! Seven thirty – you know the address.' And with that he kissed them both with damp lips – Helen squirming as his hand reached behind her and stroked the small of her back – and headed off towards the exit.

'What on earth??' exclaimed Helen when he was out of earshot. 'I can't believe you've just thrown away our evening like that?'

'Don't give me a hard time. I have no choice. Everyone is relying on me to bag another series. They'd be heart-broken if I failed – and I'd be in the shit.'

Seeing Penny's glum expression, Helen took pity on her. 'Told you we should have gone to Pizza Express.'

Penny linked arms with her friend. 'Note to self: Do not ignore advice from Helen Merrifield.'

'I still can't believe he used to be your boyfriend.'

'Boy-*fiend*, more like!'

And they enjoyed a snigger as they headed off for lunch.

*

Simon was dog-tired. His day had got off to a bad start when he realised that he should have been giving a talk on the meaning of Easter at Trevay Junior School. Unfortunately, the realisation only hit him when he was in the car, heading in the opposite direction to visit a sick parishioner in one of the hamlets beyond Pendruggan. Having shown up late and flustered for both appointments, his day had managed to get even worse when Susie Small, the local yoga teacher, called him to say that the village hall had been broken into. What with calling the police and waiting for the locksmith to arrive, Simon had once again found himself being pulled in different directions.

It was dusk by the time he made it home to the vicarage. The clouds in the sky were heavy and ominous. More bad weather had been forecast and the thought of yet another spell of torrential rain and gale-force wind only added to his gloomy mood. He hung his coat on the banister and headed to the kitchen. He was starving, but his heart sank as he opened the fridge and eyed its meagre contents. Normally, Penny would have driven to the shops in Trevay to pick something up or, as it was a Friday night, they might have headed out for a curry. Simon felt a pang. Penny would have known exactly what to say to ease his troubles and take his mind off things. He stared forlornly at the bit of old brie and half a tomato sitting on the fridge shelf. There was also a bowl of leftovers from earlier in the week, but Simon's tired brain couldn't remember what it was and the bowl of reddy-brown mush wasn't giving up its secrets.

Shutting the fridge door, he headed over to the worktop and switched on the kettle. Next to it was a note in Penny's recognisable flamboyant script:

Left you something in the freezer for every night I'm away – can't have you starving as well as drowning! Will be a better vicar's wife when I get back – promise. Pxx

Simon smiled, realising he hadn't even noticed it the

previous night before he'd staggered up to bed, to tired for anything more than a bowl of soup. Switching the kettle on, he bent down and opened the freezer. In one of the drawers was a selection of neatly packaged and labelled dishes in freezer bags: cottage pie, lasagne, spag bol and a few of pots of rhubarb crumble – his favourite.

Taking the cottage pie from the freezer he popped it in the microwave and headed out to the hallway. On the answering machine, the little red light was blinking away, and the LED display indicated that there were six new messages. He pressed the play button.

The unmistakable bossy tones of Audrey Tipton boomed out, filling the hallway:

Mrs Canter, it's Audrey here. I still haven't heard back from you regarding the Old People's Christmas Luncheon. We really must make a start on it, you know. I'll expect to hear from you as soon as you get this message. Beep.

The next one was from Margery Winthrop, one of the gaggle of pensioners who volunteered their time to help keep the church spick and span:

Hello, Penny, Margery here. Sorry to bother you but just a gentle reminder that we need to sit down and go through the spring flower rota. Doris is having her veins done and June Pearce is swanning off on a Saga cruise, so you'll need to drum up some more helpers from somewhere. Or will you put yourself down for a few shifts? Anyway, I'll try you again tomorrow. Beep.

The next one was from Emma Scott, Brown Owl of the local Brownies, who spoke in a broad Cornish accent:

Penny, my love, meant to say when I saw you last week that spring 'as sprung – so that must mean it's time to get our bums in gear for the Summer Fête. I've already had a word with Harry the scout leader, but 'e's about as much use as chocolate teapot! You'll 'ave to organise the lot of us, as usual! Bye, my lovely, speak later in the week.

Apart from a call reminding him of his dental appointment, all the other messages were in a similar vein: coffee mornings, afternoon tea for the old folks, an outing for the disabled . . . Simon couldn't figure out how Penny was able to fit it all in alongside her full-time job. He felt another pang, this time of guilt. He'd been quite cross with her about her weekend away. Why shouldn't she have a break? If he'd had to deal with this lot, he'd want to run a mile too.

He took his mobile phone out of his pocket. It was a decidedly untrendy and ancient Nokia that had been dropped, thrown and even survived a dip in a cup of tea. He'd have his trusty Nokia over a new-fangled smart phone any day.

Simon saw that he had two texts from Penny and a missed call. He'd been so busy he'd not had a chance to look at his phone all day.

He pulled Penny up from his contacts list and hit the green call button, putting the phone to his ear.

This is Penny Leighton, I can't take you call right now . . .

Simon didn't leave a message. He'd call her later. Tell her he loved her.

After he'd finished his meal, he settled himself down in front of the early evening news. *Ten minutes*, he told himself, *then I'll tackle Sunday's sermon*. Within moments, he was fast asleep.

*

Piran had been looking forward to a few hours' night fishing with his mate Brian. Their usual routine was to take the boat out, crack open a few cans and put the world to rights.

But the weather that had been threatening all day had finally broken, and as he drove through Trevay hailstones were bouncing off his battered pickup truck with such force it was like being machine-gunned with walnuts.

He let out a sigh. The weather warnings were dire for shipping and, hardy as he was, there was no way he was taking the boat out in this.

The dig at the Roman fort had been a long slog. The finds that they were turning up were incredible, but the constant battle against the elements was wearing them all down. Now that night-fishing was off the agenda, Piran wanted nothing more than to kick back with a couple of pints of Doom Bar and watch some football.

Having made sure that his little fishing boat was anchored properly in Trevay harbour – it was sure to take a battering tonight – Piran set off for the convenience store, where he planned to get some supplies in. The wind was so strong it was all he could do to open the door of his pickup. Pulling the hood of his waterproofs tighter to his face, he battled through the rain and into the store where he bought eggs, bacon, a wholemeal loaf and a couple of bottles of his favourite Cornish ale. The storm had reached biblical proportions by the time he exited the store, whistling through the narrow streets and pelting him with horizontal rain as he ran for the truck. Juggling his shopping, he struggled to find his car keys in the deep pockets of his waterproof jacket. Fumbling with wet, icy fingertips, he pulled them out, but as he did so, his single door-key was pulled along too. Piran could only watch as it spun in the air, landing with a plop in a giant puddle of rainwater that had pooled beneath his car. Letting his shopping fall, he dropped to his knees and began to scrabble around in the cold, dirty water to find it. His heart sank as his fingers made contact with the wide gaps of the storm drain. His key was gone – swept down into the sewer, never to be retrieved.

He cursed a heartfelt bollocks, retrieved his supplies and climbed back into the pickup. The only other person who had a key to his cottage was Helen, and she was too far away to be useful, but he remembered that Helen always kept a key to her own cottage underneath the flower pot in her front garden. So, grim-faced, he headed in the direction of Gull's Cry.

*

Helen and Penny were pulling up outside an imposing house on one of Kensington's most exclusive streets. They'd spent the afternoon shopping in the West End, but the sheer enjoyment of making random indulgent purchases had been dented by the knowledge that they were compelled to attend Quentin Clarkson's ghastly drinks party.

'I can't think why you went out with him in the first place. Hasn't he always been a complete and utter plonker?'

Helen looked stunning in a Cos asymmetrical dress in midnight blue which highlighted her blue eyes. Penny had gone into power dressing mode and was resplendent in an Alexander McQueen red crêpe dress that set off her blonde hair perfectly.

'Well, yes, a plonker through and through – from birth, I imagine. But underneath all that, he's got quite a fierce business brain. Before he took over, TV7 was the laughing stock of the TV world. It was all tacky game shows and bargain-bucket reality TV. Now they've got some the hottest shows on television. He was ambitious, so was I. What can I say?'

'Well, rather you than me. The guy gives me the creeps.'

Helen shuddered, remembering his hand on her back earlier that day.

'Tell me about it!' Penny lowered her voice as they approached the front door. 'You'll never guess what he used to do when we were having sex?'

'I don't think I want to know.'

'Well . . .'

But Penny never finished what she was going to say because at that moment the door flew open and standing before them was a vision in beige silk Diana Von Furstenberg.

'Penny, darling!' the vision drawled.

'Miriam. How lovely to see you, I can't believe we've left it for so long.'

Helen noticed that Penny's voice was about an octave higher than normal, which to those in the know was a clear indication that she loathed the woman.

'Do come in – and your little friend, too.' She held out an imperious hand to Helen. 'Miriam Clarkson. I'm Quentin's wife, but you'll probably recognise me from *The Lion's Lair*.'

'Yes, I thought you looked familiar.' Helen offered her hand in return but Miriam Clarkson barely touched it. *The Lion's Lair* was a hugely popular TV show where young entrepreneurs got to spend some time working alongside their business gurus. Miriam Clarkson was one of the 'Lions' and ran a multimillion-pound interior design business whose clients included Roman Abramovich and Richard Branson. She was also notoriously volatile. Helen found this odd, considering Miriam's oft-proclaimed devotion to Eastern mysticism, which she claimed helped her to 'channel the energies' of the luxury properties she was hired to imbue with her trademark style.

In person, she was stick thin, Botoxed to within an inch

of her life, and the air around her practically vibrated with a nervous energy that was enough to set your teeth on edge.

Miriam ordered a hired lackey in a crisp white-and-black uniform to take their coats, then they were shown through to an impressive reception room, awash with expensively tasteful furnishings in various shades of beige or taupe.

'Psst.' Helen nudged Penny. She'd remembered where she recognised Miriam from. 'Didn't she used to be your assistant?'

'Yep. That was why Quentin and I split up. Found him shagging her on the floor of his Canary Wharf offices.'

'That's right, it's all coming back to me now!'

'She got her talons into him pretty quickly and used his connections to build up her business. They deserve each other.'

The room was full of small groups of men and women talking, laughing and drinking. The men all wore what passed for casual in this part of London. Navy or tweed blazers from Hackett with open-necked shirts paired with mismatched chinos in salmon pink or mustard. The women seemed to share the same Knightsbridge hairdresser and wore either Burberry Prorsum or Joseph.

Quentin spotted them immediately and made a beeline for them.

'Penny, darling, so glad you could come!'

'Quentin. I see Miriam has done wonders on your pad.'

'The woman is a genius. Insisted we dug out the basement to create a Turkish hamman. The neighbours all kicked up a stink, as usual, but what Miriam wants, she usually gets! The whole place has just been Feng Shui-ed!'

'Really?' Penny raised a cynical eyebrow.

At that point, a distinguished-looking gent in his early

sixties came towards them. He had lively green eyes and an open and honest face. Helen liked him immediately.

'Penny, my dear girl! You look wonderful.'

Penny greeted him warmly with a hug and introduced him to Helen. 'Lovely to see you, too, Sir Nigel.'

'We don't often see you on the mean streets of West London,' he said. 'How is Cornish married life treating you?'

'Couldn't be better.'

'I love the place myself. The wife and I have a bolthole in St Agnes. Hope to retire there one of these days when TV7 let me out of their clutches.' He smiled at Helen apologetically. 'Do forgive me, I'm just going to borrow your friend for a few minutes, my dear. Baroness Hardy and I want to pick her brains about something . . .'

Helen gave Penny a look that said *hurry up*, then turned to find that she'd been left in the clutches of Quentin Clarkson.

'Alone at last.' He sidled up to her and placed his hand on her lower back. 'This is a big house, you know. I could take you on a little tour – there are plenty of cosy nooks and crannies that we could explore together.' His fat hand inched towards her bottom.

She was tempted to stand on his elegantly-shod toes, but before she had a chance, Miriam materialised. Her eyes were narrowed. 'What are you two talking about?' she demanded suspiciously.

'Your husband offered to take me on a private tour of the house,' Helen said innocently.

'Oh, did he now?' Miriam Clarkson's eyes narrowed with cold fury.

'Er, the Turkish hamman, darling,' spluttered Quentin. 'I thought our guests might like to see—'

Miriam didn't miss a beat. Taking Helen firmly by the arm, she said loudly, 'Let me introduce you to Camilla

45

and James. They're ordinary people just like you and I'm sure you'll have plenty in common.'

It turned out that Camilla and James both lived in Chiswick and worked for the BBC. For the next hour Helen had to listen to Camilla drone on about house prices, the difficulty in finding a parking space for their 4×4 – which had never seen a muddy field in its life – in their Chiswick Street, and how utterly selfish her Ukrainian nanny had turned out to be, asking for time off to visit her dying father in the school holidays.

'I used to live in Chiswick,' Helen said. 'But I sold up and moved to Cornwall a couple of years ago.'

Camilla looked aghast. 'But you must be kicking yourself? Your house would probably be worth twice as much by now!'

'Quite the opposite,' said Helen. 'It was the best thing I've ever done.' And with that, she excused herself, knowing that if she had stayed with those two tiresome twits for a moment longer she would scream.

Heading out onto the ambiently lit terrace. Helen took out her phone from her bag and called Piran. It went straight to voicemail. She imagined herself there instead of here, with Piran, enjoying a pint or two in the Sail Loft.

Sighing, she put her phone back in her bag and headed into the party again. She tried to catch Penny's eye, but she was in deep conversation with Sir Nigel and the Baroness and didn't notice her.

'Ah, Helen – come and meet Emily. Her son went to the same school as yours, I believe, and he's now doing an MA.' It was Camilla again.

Helen looked at her watch. Any chance of slipping away early was diminishing fast. She grabbed a cocktail and a canapé from a passing waiter and plastered a smile on her face. It was going to be a long evening.

5

It was 9.30 a.m. when Helen presented herself washed and dressed outside Penny's hotel-room door. The two women hadn't left the party until gone eleven the previous night, and by then it was far too late to retrieve their evening. They'd made it back to the hotel and were too exhausted and fed up to face anything more than a quick nightcap at the bar.

The door opened to reveal Penny in her bath robe. Helen immediately went and flopped down on the bed while Penny put the finishing touches to her make-up. Despite being the wrong side of forty, Penny's blonde hair, long legs, fair complexion and not least her infectious energy made her seem ten years younger. Simon was a lucky man, Helen thought, not for the first time.

'Were we ever as insufferable as that lot last night?' she asked Penny.

'You certainly weren't – but I've a horrible feeling that I might have been.'

'Nonsense! You've never shown the slightest sign of disappearing up your own bum like that lot. I hope I never see Quentin bloody Clarkson again.'

'I've no choice but to see him, unfortunately. But at least I'm a step closer to a new series of *Mr Tibbs*. Sir Nigel loves it – he even hinted we might be offered a long-term deal.'

'Brilliant!' Helen clapped her hands. 'And as a reward for your long-suffering and forbearing friend – i.e.: moi – today, we are going to do exactly what I say!'

'Well, OK, your majesty but it's your turn to pay for lunch.'

'It's a deal!'

*

After a light breakfast in their hotel – porridge with honey for Helen and granola and Greek yogurt for Penny – they set off towards Piccadilly station.

'Where are we going?' Penny asked.

'You'll see!'

As they headed down the escalator, the crowding seemed much worse than they remembered from the old days. *Had London always been this busy?* Helen wondered.

Their journey was a rather cramped and uncomfortable one, but they both enjoyed people-watching. Londoners kept their heads down, usually reading a paper or their Kindles. The tourists chattered loudly and took their time getting on and off the train, irritating the Londoners, who were used to a certain regimented tempo.

'Do you remember when people used to read actual books?' Helen observed.

'You're so twentieth century!'

Eventually, without too many hiccups, they reached their destination: Ladbroke Grove.

'Ah. Revisiting old haunts, are we?'

When Helen lived in London, there had been nothing she liked better than heading down to Portobello Road and rummaging around on the many hundreds of stalls for hidden treasures. You never knew what you might turn up. Helen had, in her time, found an Art Nouveau mirror from the Morris school; a Clarice Cliff milk jug and even a vivid green Whitefriars vase. Her move to Cornwall had been a new start and she'd jettisoned many of her belongings, but those cherished items still had pride of place in Gull's Cry.

They headed slowly up the Portobello Road. It was heaving with tourists and locals. Fashionable young men and women spilled out of the trendy cafés and funky coffee shops. When Helen had first started going there, all the shops had a distinctly home-made feel. Now High Street brands jostled for attention. Gone were the conspicuous shaggy-haired musicians and trustafarians, making way for hordes of rich, successful Londoners.

Stopping at a stall selling crockery, china and bric-a-brac, Helen spotted an adorable honey pot. She picked it up and scrutinised it. No scratches or chips, and looking at the bottom she could see that it was from the Crown Devon factory. It would look lovely on the kitchen windowsill of her cottage.

'How much?' she asked the stallholder.

Despite being surrounding by London's fashionable set, the trader was definitely old-school.

'Forty quid, love.'

'Eh? That's extortionate!'

'Blame eBay, love, not me. That's the going rate.'

'Rubbish, you could find something like this in the Sue Ryder shop in Trevay for a couple of quid.'

'Look, love, I dunno what the 'ell or where the 'ell this Trevay is, but down the Portobella, it's forty quid.'

He leaned into her confidingly. 'Tell you what, gimme thirty and you've got yerself a bargain.'

Despite knowing she was being ripped off, Helen found

herself reaching for her purse and handing the money over. The trader wrapped her little honey pot in a bit of old newspaper and tipped his beanie hat at her.

'Pleasure doing business wiv ya!'

Helen muttered under her breath, 'Bloody shyster.' But she was secretly pleased with her cute pot and wrapped it up in her scarf to make sure it was quite safe.

*

Eventually, after stopping off for Penny to purchase a grey kid leather biker jacket in All Saints, they reached Notting Hill Gate itself. You could tell you were higher up as the wind caught their hair and gave them a wind-swept appearance.

'There's a farmer's market around here somewhere.' Helen took out her iPhone and Google-mapped their location. 'This way!' They both headed off towards one of the backstreets, soon coming to a car park where a dozen or more stalls were selling their wares. Cheese, cured meats, home-made curry pastes and much more were on sale, and the smell of a hog roast filled their nostrils, making their tummies grumble.

'Oooh look!' exclaimed Penny, pointing to a stall selling Cornish pasties and sausage rolls. 'I could murder one of those!'

They headed over and Penny asked for two Cornish pasties.

'Sure,' answered the friendly girl behind the counter. She was wearing a woolly hat and giant cardy; even though it was April, there was still a chill in the air. She put them in separate bags. 'That's ten pounds, please.'

'What??' Penny spluttered. 'Five pounds each?? Are they filled with gold dust?'

'Sorry. I don't set the prices,' the girl explained apologetically.

Penny handed the money over and then said to Helen incredulously, 'But in Queenie's, they're ninety pence.'

'We're not in Kansas any more, Toto,' Helen informed her.

They munched on their pasties hungrily, but both decided – out of earshot of the nice young girl – that they weren't a patch on Queenie's, with her lovely shorter-than-short pastry and meaty, peppery filling.

'Got any room left?' asked Helen.

'Possibly. What have you got in mind?'

'There's a Pizza Express round the corner.'

'Go on then. That pasty was just an hors d'oeuvre!' And they headed off for second lunch.

*

After a delicious lunch of shared pizza and dough balls, the two women decided to head back to their hotel. Both were tired after spending all morning on their feet and so they decided to spend the afternoon indulging themselves; Helen had a pedi and a facial while Penny luxuriated in a two-hour full-body citrus wrap with pressure-point massage and scalp treatment. It was bliss and her shoulder was feeling better already.

As Helen was calling the shots, she'd insisted that they spend the evening at their favourite London hang-out, Mortimer's Champagne and Oyster Bar in the heart of Mayfair.

'Where to?' the cabbie asked as they jumped in his sleek black vehicle.

'Upper Grosvenor Street, please,' said Penny.

'Any word from Simon?' Helen asked.

'I've tried to speak to him, but we've missed each other. I had a missed call from him but he didn't leave a message, and there was no answer when I rang back.' Penny looked anxious. 'I hope he's not giving me the silent treatment. I couldn't bear it. Maybe we shouldn't have come.'

'Don't be silly, he's just busy, that's all. I'm sure he'll call.'

'Perhaps you're right. What about Piran?'

Helen let out an irritated sigh. 'Oh, he'll be completely wrapped up in his beloved Roman fort. I've given up!'

They stared silently out of the window, each with their own thoughts, taking in the Saturday-night crowds thronging the streets. Before long they had reached the exclusive Mayfair Street lined with stylish bars and restaurants. They pulled up outside Mortimer's and the first thing that they saw was a rope barrier, behind which was a queue of people waiting to enter the bar.

'Don't seem to remember queuing to get into Mortimer's,' said Penny.

'Nor me. There used to be a nice old gent who opened the door for you – where's he gone?'

In his place were two imposing-looking men in bomber jackets with shaved heads and earpieces. Next to them was a small, fierce young woman wearing a tight-fitting black sequined dress and brandishing a clipboard.

Helen and Penny joined the queue. In front of them was a glittering assortment of young, beautiful people. The women wore the tiniest of dresses and there was plenty of cleavage and midriff on display. *Where are their coats?* Penny wondered.

'Look at her heels!' Helen pointed at a pretty girl in

front of them who was teetering on a pair of Louboutins that were at least six inches high.

'Ridiculous,' observed Penny.

The queue was moving quickly and before long they had reached the girl with the clipboard.

'Names?' she demanded.

'I beg your pardon?'

'Your names? I need to check you're on the list,' she snapped, eyeing them both with disdain.

The women looked at each other in bafflement.

'What list?'

'Look,' the woman almost barked at them, 'this is an exclusive club and we can't just let anybody in. If your names are not on my list, then there's no entry.'

At this point Helen was tempted to turn around and head off to the nearest pub, but Penny loved a challenge. Besides, she was damned if she was going to be beaten by this brash and obnoxious young woman. Her animal instincts sparked into action.

'Oh, I think there must be some mistake. I'm Penny Leighton, Head of Penny Leighton Productions? We're got a private table booked. Jemima and Russell are coming – they're on your list, aren't they? And Beatrice and Eugenie? You've got them down too, right?

The girl looked at her list and said uncertainly, 'Well . . . I'm not sure . . .'

'There'll be trouble if they arrive and we're not there. Hey, I'm just thinking – there's something about you. I'm casting for a new reality series set in a London Club. You look like exactly the sort of person we're looking for.'

'Really?' She had the girl's attention now. After a moment, weighing things up, she seemed to reach a decision.

'OK, give me your business card.' Penny obliged and

the girl popped it onto her clipboard. She nodded to one of the bouncers, who opened up the red-rope gate and let them through.

Once inside, Helen and Penny's jaws hit the floor. The Mortimer's they remembered had epitomised quiet, understated elegance; now all they could see was a throng of people shouting to be heard above the loud music and flashing neon lights.

They looked at each other in dismay. Instead of waiters in black uniforms working the room with calm efficiency, the bar and the tables were being served by thin young women in short miniskirts and low-cut tops.

'Do we even dare have a drink? This place is making me feel really old,' said Helen.

'Come on, we've got this far. Let's have just the one and then we'll bugger off.'

They seated themselves at one of the tables and immediately a scantily clad young woman arrived to take their order.

'What can I get you, ladies?' the girl asked in an Eastern European accent.

'Two glasses of champagne, please,' said Penny.

'Of course.' The girl gave them a friendly smile.

'Can I ask you something?' Penny enquired of the girl. 'What happened to the old Mortimer's? The place is so um . . . different from the last time we came.'

The girl leaned in towards them to make herself heard above the music.

'It was bought out by big Russian businessman. He change everything and make us wear these clothes to attract rich big spenders.'

'Well, it seems to be working.' Penny looked around her at the clientele.

'Sometimes the men take it too far,' the girl continued, 'but the tips are good. I will get you your drinks.'

Within a few minutes she was back. While the bill was extortionate, the champagne was good.

Helen raised the glass to her lips and was just about to toast Penny when the words died on her lips.

'Oh no.'

'What?' Penny turned to see what Helen was looking at. Sitting at a table adjacent to theirs were Helen's ex-husband Gray, and his new girlfriend, the actress Dahlia Darling. Dahlia was of indeterminate age, but had once been the Purdy of her generation. She and Gray had been an item for a while now, having met on the set of *Mr Tibbs* and Helen suspected that her vain, selfish and serially unfaithful ex had got himself more than he bargained for.

Dahlia spotted them first. Grabbing Gray's hand, she headed over to their table. She was charm personified and if she felt any awkwardness or jealously at Helen's presence, she was far too regal and professional ever to let on. Helen, for her part, felt nothing but joy that Gray was now somebody else's problem.

'Darlings!!' Dhalia greeted them effusively and demanded that the waitress bring them more champagne.

Gray gave them both a hug and Helen was sure he held her for longer than was strictly necessary.

'We're meeting my agent and his wife – we're out celebrating because I've just managed to get a cameo in *Downton*!'

'That's thrilling!' said Penny. 'Just make sure that you're free for the next series of *Mr Tibbs* – it wouldn't be the same without you.'

'Don't you worry, my darling. I wouldn't miss it for the world, would I, Gray?' Dahlia threw herself at his neck and gave him a fulsome kiss on the cheek. As she did so, he pointedly locked eyes with Helen and threw her one of his 'puppy-dog left out in the rain' looks that she knew so well.

They chatted, laughed and shared old jokes, enjoying Dahlia's anecdotes despite the noisy surroundings. After a while Helen excused herself to go downstairs to the Ladies. There were mirrors everywhere and she felt like Alice in Wonderland as she was assailed by vision after vision of herself reflected into infinity. Disconcertingly, when she sat down on the toilet seat she was horrified to see herself reflected mid-wee. *Whoever thought this was a good idea?* she wondered, and deduced that it was bound to be a man.

Heading towards the stairs, she hoped that they would be able to leave soon. They had a table booked at Chez Walter and she was finding the club and the company of Gray and Dahlia rather wearing. She thought longingly of Pendruggan.

As she reached the stairwell, her heart sank as she saw Gray heading down the stairs towards her.

'Helen, darling, you look ravishing. How are you, you look a bit sad – are you?'

'No Gray, you're projecting – I'm perfectly happy, thank you!'

'I don't believe you. I've done nothing but dream about you for months. How could you throw something so good away? Come on, Helen, you know how good we were together.'

He took her hand and moved as close to her as he could in the confined space of the stairwell. His face was inches from hers.

'The grass not so green on the other side, Gray? The only person who threw anything away was you. You didn't seem to want the vow of fidelity, but I can honestly say that I've never been happier – you did me a favour! I wish you and Dahlia well – you make a lovely couple!'

And with that, she extricated herself from his clutches and tripped back up the stairs.

'Come on, Penny, it's time to go,' she said when she reached their table, interrupting Penny mid-flow. 'We've got a date with a man called Walter. Dahlia, remind Gray it's Sean's birthday next week, won't you!'

'Hold your horses!' Penny downed the rest of her Bollinger and sprinted out after Helen into the night.

6

It was Sunday. They'd treated themselves to a fry-up for breakfast before heading off to Paddington to catch their train. Not a sleeper this time, and they had a five-hour journey ahead of them, but they'd stocked up with the Sunday papers and plenty of Haribos and had now ensconced themselves in First Class.

'I can't believe we managed to run into all those people. You know, the ones we'd rather not see.'

'Well, they do call it London Village. It's worse than Pendruggan!'

'I'm glad were going back. I'm not sure London is quite what I remembered,' said Helen. 'Perhaps we're not really Londoners any more?'

'But they say that when a woman is tired of London, she's tired of life.'

'Well, I never heard anyone in Cornwall say that,' Helen responded.

'But we're not really Cornish – and we never will be. Look at Queenie: she's lived in Pendruggan for five decades and they *still* think of her as an outsider.

'That's probably because she still sounds like a Billingsgate fishwife!'

'True!' laughed Penny.

'I hate to ask, but did you hear from Simon yet?'

Penny looked apprehensive. 'No. Today's impossible

because he'll be conducting services all day. I'm afraid even if he could get to the phone he wouldn't call. He's still peeved with me.'

'I'm sure he isn't. Simon isn't one to harbour resentments,' Helen reassured her.

'Perhaps not. But maybe he was right: I should have stayed in Pendruggan and helped out.'

'Everything will be fine. You'll see.'

*

They reached Truro in the late afternoon and the journey back to Pendruggan passed without incident. The bad weather had blown over and the coastline was bathed in a magnificent sunset; the sky ablaze with vivid purple and orange hues.

'Red sky at night,' said Penny.

She dropped Helen at the village green, by the gate to Gull's Cry. They gave each other a big hug.

'Thanks for coming with me,' said Penny sincerely. 'It may not have been the weekend we expected but it has certainly made me appreciate what I've got.'

'I'd have been furious if you'd asked anyone else!'

'You'll be at the blessing of the tower in Trevay on Tuesday?'

'I'll be there with bells on!' Helen joked.

'Very funny!'

Helen pushed the little gate open and waved to Penny. Then she turned to face Gull's Cry.

What she saw almost took her breath away. Outside the cottage, Gasping Bob's wiry brown body was on top of the ladder, fixing some heavy tarpaulin to the roof. He turned around and waved to her from above, making a noise that sounded like one of his 'Ah's. She waved back at him, delighted that something was finally being done to sort the roof out.

The door of the cottage opened and out came Piran, trowel in hand. His hair was covered in flecks of white plaster and paint.

Despite the risk of denting his reputation as the grumpiest man in Cornwall, Helen threw herself into his arms. He was still *her* grumpiest man in Cornwall, after all.

'Careful now, maid.' He held the dirty trowel away from her, and Helen could tell from the light in his eyes that he was pleased to see her too. 'How was the big smoke?'

'Great,' she answered, rather too quickly. Then her eyes turned to Gasping Bob. 'At last! Something is being done about the leaks. Not that I'm complaining, of course!'

Piran looked sheepish. 'Lost my key last night, had to sleep here.'

Helen smiled. 'Ah . . . Not very nice, is it?'

'Yeah, well. Spent all night bailing out. Sorry, Helen. I was a bit caught up in meself. Should have sorted it before now. But I've repaired the plaster up there, and Bob thinks the roof should be sorted in a couple of days.'

'Good old Bob. He's a sight for sore eyes.' She surveyed Bob's skin-tight shorts and narrow bum. 'Well, he's a sight, anyway.'

'Don't let him hear you say that – he's got quite a rep with the ladies.'

Helen laughed and kissed Piran's nose, plaster and all. 'Cornish men! There's no one like you!'

They made their way inside the house and Helen dropped her bags by the door.

'Home sweet home,' she said, meaning every word. 'How are things at the Roman fort?'

'I've got something to show you,' he said.

He went over to his big overcoat and took something out of the pocket. A shy look in his eye, he handed it to Helen. It was something small but quite heavy and wrapped in tissue paper.

'What is it?'

''urry up and open it!' he urged. 'But be careful.'

'All right, all right!' Helen teased open the tissue paper and caught her breath as she saw what lay inside. It was a silver coin, tinged with green and bent and battered at the edges. Helen could tell it was very old but remarkably well-preserved. On the 'heads' side was what appeared to be a Roman head and the words 'Claudius Caesar'.

She looked at Piran quizzically.

'The Roman Emperor, Claudius. We found it a couple of weeks ago. Turn it over.'

On the other side was a depiction of a woman. Helen couldn't make any of the writing out but the woman definitely had a strong Roman nose.

'Who is she?' she asked.

'We think it's Helen of Troy.'

Helen's eyes were like saucers, 'Really?'

'Yep. One of the archaeologists found this and I thought of you.'

'Oh, Piran. It's wonderful. Is this for me?'

'Yes and no. It's now owned by the Crown, but I've spoken to a silversmith in Trevay and she's made you a replica to wear on a necklace. We can pick it up tomorrow.'

'Piran Ambrose, I think that is the single most romantic thing any man has ever done for me.'

'Well,' he smiled, his eyes twinkling. 'Just keep it to yourself.'

*

The great and the good of Trevay and Pendruggan had turned out in force to see the blessing of the new bell tower. Penny and Helen, who hadn't seen each other since their return on Sunday evening, shuffled along one of the rows near the front. Simon had already taken his place next to Louise, the outgoing vicar. The bishop, fresh from his retreat, would be officiating at today's ceremony.

As she sat down, Penny caught the eye of Audrey Tipton in the next row, who gave her a stiff nod of the head.

'She's still miffed about the Great Pendruggan Bake-Off. Queenie reckons that we're the odds-on favourites to win!' she whispered, gleefully.

'Never mind that, how are things at home? Simon?'

'Shush, the bishop's about to speak.'

The bishop welcomed them all and then, after a short prayer, addressed the congregation.

'It's a pleasure to be here today to bless this wonderful new bell tower. The builders have done an excellent job and I'm sure I speak for us all when I say that Simon here has moved heaven and earth to make sure that everything ran on time and on budget, all while trying to run his own ministry as well as keeping everything afloat here. I think we owe him a big thank you.'

The gathered parishioners gave Simon a round of warm applause and the bishop encouraged him to step up to the dais and say a few words. After thanking the verger and the army of helpers who had turned out to lend a hand, he addressed his wife.

'I just want to say how much I owe to my wife, Penny. She's the one who gives me all the love and support I need to carry out my duties. She's the one who really should get a round of applause.' The parishioners clapped her heartily and Penny blushed as Simon said, 'Thank you, Penny. I'm so glad to have you home.' His eyes shone with love for her.

The bishop said another short prayer of blessing, and across Trevay – from the church all the way to the Pavilions Theatre near the harbour – the bells rang out crisp and clear throughout the town.

A shaft of light filtered through the stained-glass windows and shone down on the happy group of friends, Helen of Troy glimmering in its dappled sunshine.

A Seaside
Affair

1

'You should've woken me, silly.' Ryan Hearst ambled into the sunny kitchen, scratching himself somewhere inside his rumpled boxer shorts.

His girlfriend, Jess Tate, glanced up from reading the paper at the kitchen table and allowed her eyebrows to wrinkle briefly in distaste.

Ryan bent down and gave her a kiss on her freckled nose. A small gesture he was prone to, which always managed to irritate her.

'What's for breakfast?' He stretched out his muscular arms, then straightened up and yawned. His armpits gave off an unpleasant odour.

Jess pushed up her reading specs, sweeping her loose brown curls off her face, and gave him what she hoped was a relaxed smile. 'If your fans could see you now . . .'

'Yeah, don't tell them. Anyway, baby, I'm all yours.' He placed his hands either side of her head and thrust his hips and crotch towards her, mimicking a male stripper. She pulled a face and turned away. 'You pong. Go and have a shower and I'll make something to eat.'

'You love me, baby, you know you do.' He scratched his chest and yawned again. 'I've missed you, Jess. I really have.'

She looked into his dark, almond-shaped eyes, even more sexy with the tanned creases of crow's feet at their edges.

'Yes, and I've missed you,' she murmured, closing her eyes and forming her full lips into a shape for kissing – but he was already on his way to the bathroom.

With a sigh she got up and made her way to the fridge. There were plenty of eggs, a slab of cheese and some mushrooms. Ryan hadn't touched a carbohydrate since the third person in their relationship, Cosmo Venini, had entered their lives.

'Will an omelette do you?' she called. But he couldn't hear her over the sound of the shower.

Two pairs of beady eyes popped up over the dog basket next to the dishwasher.

Jess bent down to tickle a brace of plump tummies. 'Daddy's home, girls.'

Elsie and Ethel were miniature dachshund sisters. Ryan had brought them home nine months ago, the day he had landed the title role in *Venini*, a TV series about the exploits of a globe-trotting classical conductor who moonlights as an MI5 agent. The show had been an overnight success and as a result the tabloids had given Ryan the dubious honour of dubbing him 'the thinking woman's brioche'.

Jess recalled that cold January afternoon when he'd poked his head round the living room door, the smell of frosty air clinging to him. She was huddled on the sofa in front of the TV, swaddled from head to toe in their duvet to combat the lack of heating, watching *Deal or No Deal* and wondering whether she should apply to be a contestant in the hope of bringing home some prize money. One look at Ryan's face told her his audition had been successful.

'Oh my God! You got the job?' The icy temperature forgotten, she'd thrown off the duvet and leapt up from the sofa.

'Yep. Call me Cosmo!' He pushed the door wide open and stood in front of her, smiling self-deprecatingly, still wearing the huge misshapen tweed overcoat that he'd bought in the charity shop the previous winter.

For a moment Jess could only jump up and down on the spot, beside herself with happiness, then she ran across the room, hugged him tightly and kissed him. 'I'm so happy for you! This is *it*, Ryan! This is your big break – oh my God, oh my God – we can pay the gas bill!'

'I think perhaps we can!' he laughed, pulling her closer to him. 'Oh . . .' He loosened his grip on her and created a little space between them, 'Almost forgot – I've bought you a present to celebrate.'

She smiled, wide-eyed with excitement, thinking of the silver earrings she'd pointed out to him the previous weekend. 'You mustn't, Ryan. We don't have any money yet.'

He opened his coat and rummaged in the deep poacher's pockets within.

'Ta-dah!' His hands emerged clutching two long bodies with impossibly short legs.

'What the hell . . .?' These were not earrings. 'Who are they for?'

'You.'

'Why?'

'Present.'

'I don't need a present. My present is you getting this great job.' In spite of herself she reached out and tickled a pair of silken ears. 'When does shooting start?'

'In a couple of days.'

'Gosh, that's quick. Where?' Jess asked.

'Northumberland.'

'A bit of a schlep from Willesden.'

'Yeah . . . Then Milan, New York and Hong Kong.'

She stopped the tickling and looked at Ryan.

'For how long?'

'Six months.' His eyes dropped to the two warm, wriggling pups.

Jess pushed her hair behind her ears, suddenly feeling all of her pleasure at the news drain away. 'Six months? But you will be coming home, won't you? Backwards and forwards?'

Ryan shook his head, 'Probably not.'

'Oh,' said Jess, suddenly deflated.

He held the puppies up and spoke to them: 'So that's where you two come in. You're going to look after Mummy while Daddy's gone.'

Now she got it. The dogs were her consolation prize. A way of keeping her occupied while Ryan was away having the time of his life.

'So you get to swan off and I'm left holding the fort here, on my own? And it isn't only that, Ryan – pets are such a tie.' She was aware of the whining note that had crept into her voice. 'Suppose I get a job that means *I* have to go away? Who'll look after them then?'

He set the dogs down and she heard their little tappy claws on the tiles as he put his arms around her. She clung to him and inhaled the distinctive smell of his coat, burying herself in his neck.

'Don't be like that, Jess. I'm really trying here. Don't spoil it for me.'

*

Ryan ran the soap over his body and revelled in his newly honed physique. His personal trainer, insisted upon by the production company, had worked him hard but it was definitely worth it. Biceps, triceps, abs, quads, arse. Not bad for a forty-two-year-old. There was no doubt about it: men were luckier than women. The older they got the better they looked. George Clooney, Richard Gere – even Sean Connery in his eighties. For women it was tougher, and everyone in the business knew it. Helen Mirren and Meryl Streep were the exceptions. Poor Jess; she would struggle to find work now, unless it was playing a worn-down mum, or a character role.

Ryan got out of the shower and wrapped a large bath sheet around his waist. He checked himself out in the mirror then pulled the towel a little lower to show off the muscled definition of his hips, stomach and groin. Donning his 'Cosmo' face he gave his reflection a seductive grin and growled, 'Down, boy! It's only me, silly.'

*

Ryan loved going out in public. He always wore his film-star-in-disguise sunglasses and a baseball cap. The thrill of being recognised hadn't left him yet. Today, walking the dogs on a busy Hampstead Heath, he felt as if he owned the world. *Venini* was top of the ratings, his face was on the cover of *Esquire* magazine, he had just been voted the Sexiest Man in Britain and it looked as if the Best Actor BAFTA was sure to have his name on it. Beside him, Jess was recounting what he thought was a rather tedious and seemingly interminable story about her agent and a part in a commercial she'd been put up for the previous week.

'. . . I wouldn't have cared if she'd told me they were looking for actresses ten years older than me. I would have dressed the part. But then to go and be told that I looked *too* middle-aged, without even trying, it was just so humiliating . . . Ethel, come away from the ducks! I mean, do I really look middle-aged? My CV says thirty-eight! Where do these advertising execs, fresh out of junior school, think middle age begins? Twenty-five? . . . Elsie, come away from the Labrador, he's too big for you! Honestly, Ryan, maybe I should start thinking about a bit of Botox or getting my hair cut or dyed. What do you think?'

But before Ryan had a chance to respond they were interrupted by something that was becoming an ever-more regular occurrence.

'Cosmo! Cosmo Venini! It is you, isn't it?'

An over-made-up woman in her fifties was power-walking towards Ryan, who had stopped and was taking off his sunglasses, wrinkling his beautiful eyes into a smile. He held his hands out in a gesture of surrender.

She arrived, puffing slightly, and all but elbowed Jess out of the way in her eagerness to accost Ryan.

'I knew it was you! What's your real name again, I've forgotten?'

Only Jess knew the slight tightness at the corner of Ryan's lips signalled annoyance.

'George Clooney,' he replied, oozing charm. The woman laughed hysterically as if this was the funniest thing she'd ever heard. He held his hand out to her. 'It's Ryan, Ryan Hearst. And you are . . .?'

'Gilly. Gilly Lomax. I live over there—' She pointed to a pretty pink house just outside the railings of the park. 'You're always welcome to pop in.'

'I'm afraid he's very busy.' Jess stepped in. 'I'm his partner.'

'The kettle's always on . . .' Gilly continued talking to Ryan. 'I think you're marvellous, and all those gorgeous locations you film in. Venice is my favourite. I've been to the Teatro La Fenice, it's so romantic!'

'Ryan, we must go, the dogs are getting tired.' Jess tugged at his jacket sleeve. Not some old charity-shop jacket, but a Prada summer collection number that had cost thousands.

'Sorry, darling.' He smiled at Jess and draped his arm across her shoulders in a show of ownership.

'Oh.' The woman swept a look over Jess, from to top bottom, then returned to Ryan. 'Perhaps your friend wouldn't mind taking a photo of us both on my phone.' She pulled it from her pocket and pushed it into Jess's hand. 'Take a few. Close up.'

'Of course.' Jess watched grimly as the woman cosied up to a willing Ryan, and then proceeded to take a series of photos where she knew the woman either had her eyes shut or her mouth at an unflattering angle. Just for good measure, she made sure the last couple of snaps were out of focus.

'Oh, they're perfect!' she announced, quickly turning the phone off and handing it back before the ghastly Gilly could look at them. 'Lovely to meet you. Come on, Ryan.'

*

They arrived at the park café during a lull between waves of pushchairs, toddlers and exhausted-looking parents. Having bought their coffees they steered their way through the plastic tables until they found a relatively unsticky one in the sunshine. Jess tied Elsie and Ethel's leads to her chair and sat down gratefully.

Ryan took a sip of the scalding and bitter cappuccino then reached over and squeezed Jess's hand. 'That poor woman. I can't believe you could be so mean. You'll have ruined her day.'

'Well, it made mine. Rude cow. I'm invisible to your fans. They push past me and tread on my toes to get to you. No wonder casting agents reject me – I'm invisible.'

Ryan had heard this lament often enough to know where it was going. He tried to head it off at the pass.

'Not to me you're not.'

'Really?'

'You're my girl.'

'Am I?'

'You sure are.' He took her other hand and gazed soulfully into her eyes, hoping it would have the desired effect.

'Even when you're away with all those gorgeous actresses?' Jess peered at him intently. 'You can tell me the truth, you know. Are you sure you're not tempted?'

'No,' he lied. 'You know me better than that,' he protested, as if wounded by the accusation.

'I thought I knew you,' she said, her voice wavering, 'but that was before . . .'

Oh, not this again, thought Ryan. He pulled one hand away from hers and swept it through the floppy long hair he'd been cultivating for Cosmo.

'Darling, that was five years ago. We are over that, aren't we? I can't believe I was such a fool and nearly lost you. Besides, can you imagine the bad press if I did that now and someone found out?'

This time it was Jess who pulled her hand away.

'That's nice. You're more concerned about the damage to your image than the hurt it would cause me.'

'That's not what I meant,' Ryan sighed, tired of Jess's insecurities. 'What you need is a job. A good job. One that will give you back your confidence. You're a great actress – the best. You're beautiful and clever and—'

'Unemployable.'

Knowing he would have to choose his words carefully or else this would escalate into a full-blown row, Ryan tried to buy himself some thinking time by picking up his cup and taking two large mouthfuls of coffee. Clearly in no mood to let him off the hook, Jess fixed him with a flinty glare and allowed the uncomfortable silence to drag on, broken only by the tap-tap-tap of her foot against the chair leg.

A sudden inspiration came to Ryan's rescue: 'Look, I've got two weeks off before we start filming the second series of *Venini*. Suppose you and I take a break . . .?'

'Where?'

'How about Thailand? Stay in one of those wonderful spas. Beauty treatments, exercise classes, sunshine . . . We could rent a little hut perched on stilts over the sea, just the two of us, no distractions.'

'I can't afford it.'

'My treat.'

'But I hate living off you.'

Ryan sighed in exasperation, 'Can't I treat you?'

'We'll have to put the girls in kennels, and that's expensive.'

'Oh for God's sake, Jess! The two of us are going on a bloody holiday and you'll bloody well like it – OK?'